Welcome to The Giggle Club

The Giggle Club is a collecti⟨...⟩ books made to put a giggle into early reading. There are funny stories about a contrary mouse, a dancing fox, a turtle with a trumpet, a pig with a ball, a hungry monster, a laughing lobster, an elephant who sneezes away the jungle and lots more! Each of these characters is a member of **The Giggle Club**, but anyone can join: just pick up a **Giggle Club** book, read it and get giggling!

Turn to the checklist on the inside back cover and tick off the Giggle Club books you have read.

TEE HEE!

HA HA!

For Joe

First published 1995 by Walker Books Ltd
87 Vauxhall Walk, London SE11 5HJ

This edition published 1997

10 9 8 7 6 5 4

© 1995 Anita Jeram

This book has been typeset in Columbus.

Printed in Hong Kong

British Library Cataloguing in Publication Data
A catalogue record for this book is
available from the British Library.

ISBN 0-7445-4782-2

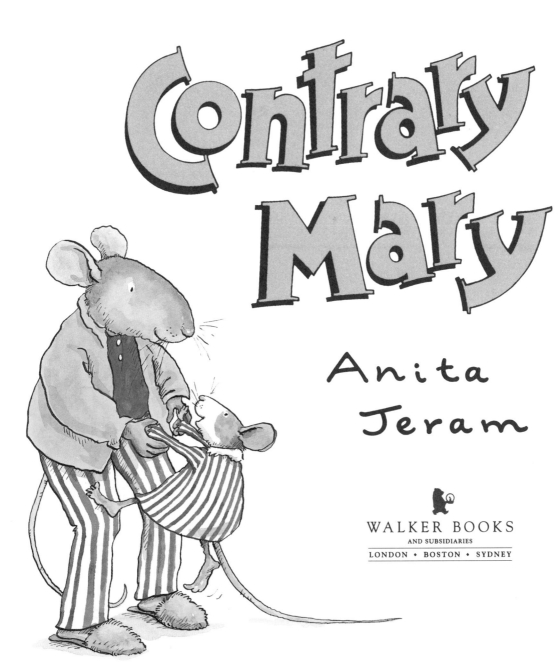

Contrary Mary

Anita Jeram

WALKER BOOKS
AND SUBSIDIARIES
LONDON • BOSTON • SYDNEY

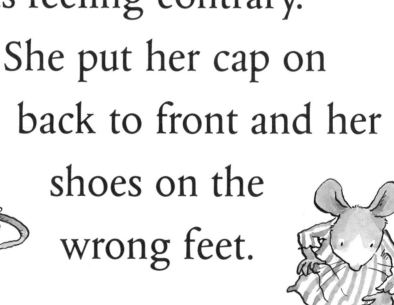

When Mary got up this morning she was feeling contrary. She put her cap on back to front and her shoes on the wrong feet.

"Are you awake, Mary?"
her mum called.
"No!" said Contrary Mary.

For breakfast there
was hot toast with
peanut butter.
"What would you like,
Mary?" asked Mum.
"Roast potatoes and gravy,
please," said Contrary Mary.

When they went
to the shops,
it was raining.

"Come under
the umbrella, Mary,"
said Mum.
But Contrary Mary
didn't. She just danced
about, getting wet.

All day long,
Contrary Mary did
contrary things.
She rode her
bicycle, backwards.
She went for
a walk,
on her hands.

She read a book upside
down. She flew her
kite along the ground.
Mary's mum shook her head.
"Mary, Mary, quite
contrary," she said.
And then she
had an idea.

That evening,
at bedtime, instead of
tucking Mary in the right
way round, Mary's mum
tucked her in upside down.

Then she opened
the curtains,
turned on the
light, kissed Mary's
toes and said,
"Good morning!"

Mary laughed
and laughed.
"Contrary Mum!"
she said.

"Do you love me, Contrary Mary?" asked Mary's mum, giving her a cuddle.

"No!" said
Contrary Mary.
And she gave
her mum a
great big kiss.

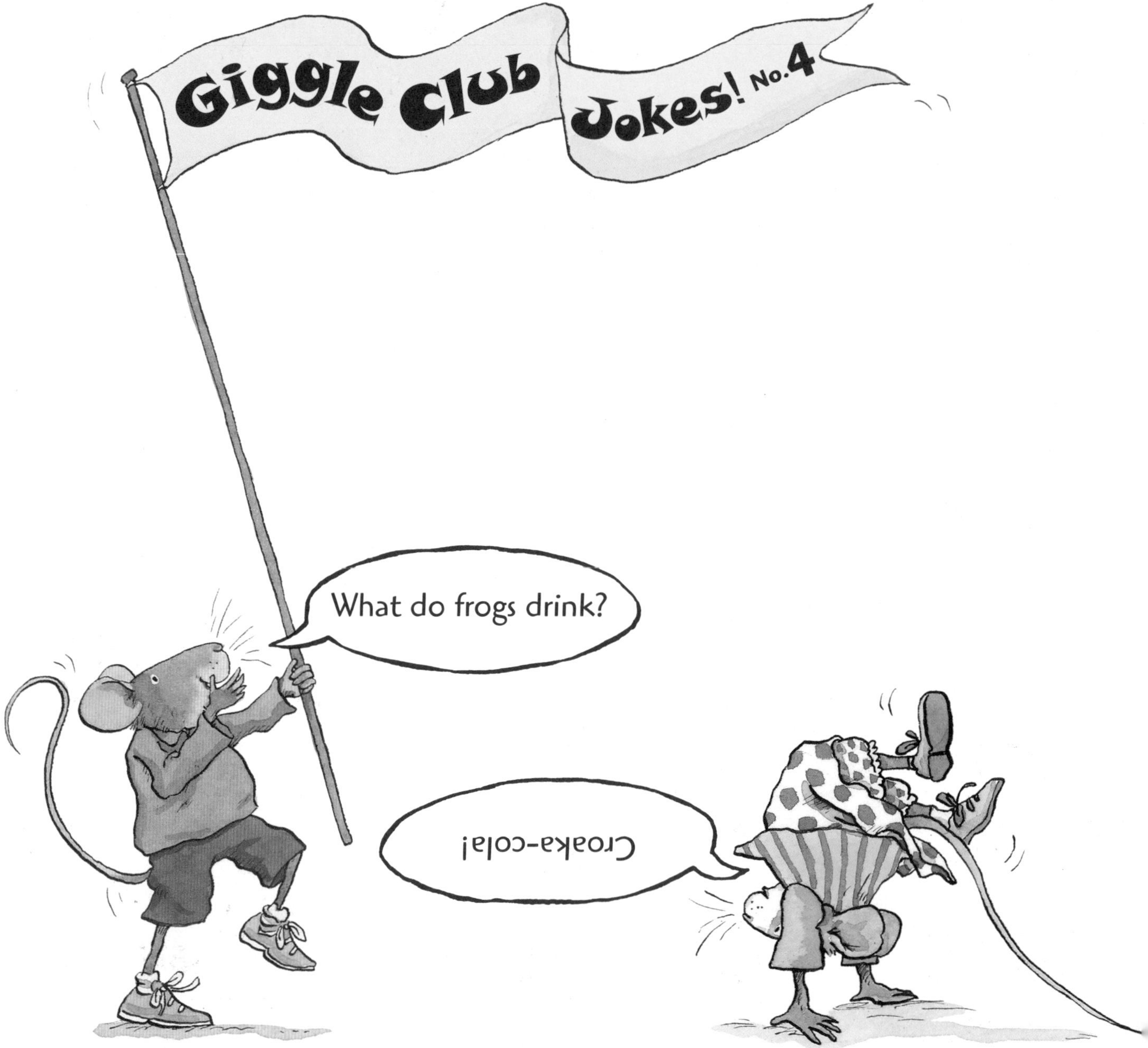
Giggle Club Jokes! No.4
What do frogs drink?
Croaka-cola!